MRS. WHITE RABBIT

Written and illustrated by

Gilles Bachelet

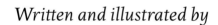

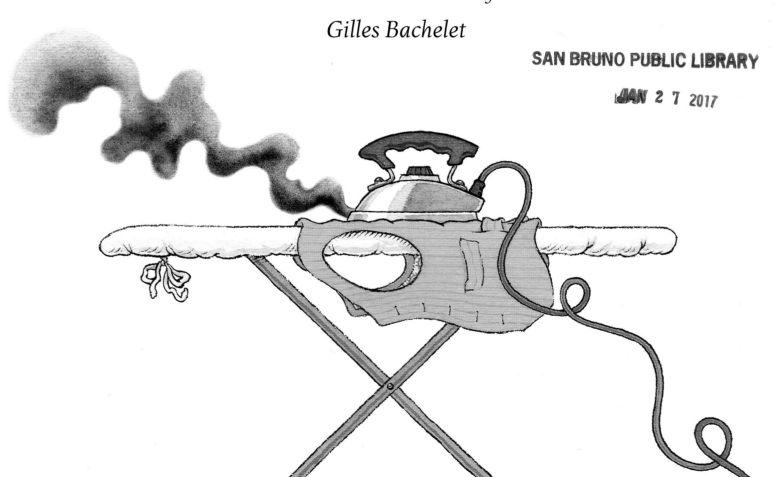

EERDMANS BOOKS
FOR YOUNG READERS
GRAND RAPIDS, MICHIGAN

GILLES BACHELET has been creating picture books since 2002 and currently works as a freelance illustrator in Paris. His previous books include *My Cat, the Silliest Cat in the World* and *When the Silliest Cat was Small* (both Abrams).

For Patrick, to whom I owe so much.
For Mireille, whose birthday I sometimes forget.
With my most humble apologies to Mr. Lewis Carroll.

— G. B.

First published in the United States in 2017 by Eerdmans Books for Young Readers,
an imprint of Wm. B. Eerdmans Publishing Co.
2140 Oak Industrial Drive N.E., Grand Rapids, Michigan 49505
www.eerdmans.com/youngreaders

Originally published in France under the title Madame le Lapin Blanc © Éditions du seuil, 2012

Manufactured at Tien Wah Press in Malaysia.

17 18 19 20 21 22   8 7 6 5 4 3 2 1

A catalog record of this book is available from the Library of Congress.

ISBN 978-0-8028-5483-4

The display type was set in Modern No. 20
The text type was set in Edita and Modern No. 20

My dear diary,

Phew!

After stamping his feet, champing at the bit, grumbling, moaning, ranting — all because I hadn't ironed his waistcoat well enough — my husband has finally decided to go to work. Late, as always.

I will take this brief moment of peace and quiet to give you some news. Ever since we moved here, I've hardly had time to confide my worries, my problems, and my few moments of happiness to you.

Beatrix, our eldest daughter, worries me a lot.
In the past, she wanted to be a housewife.

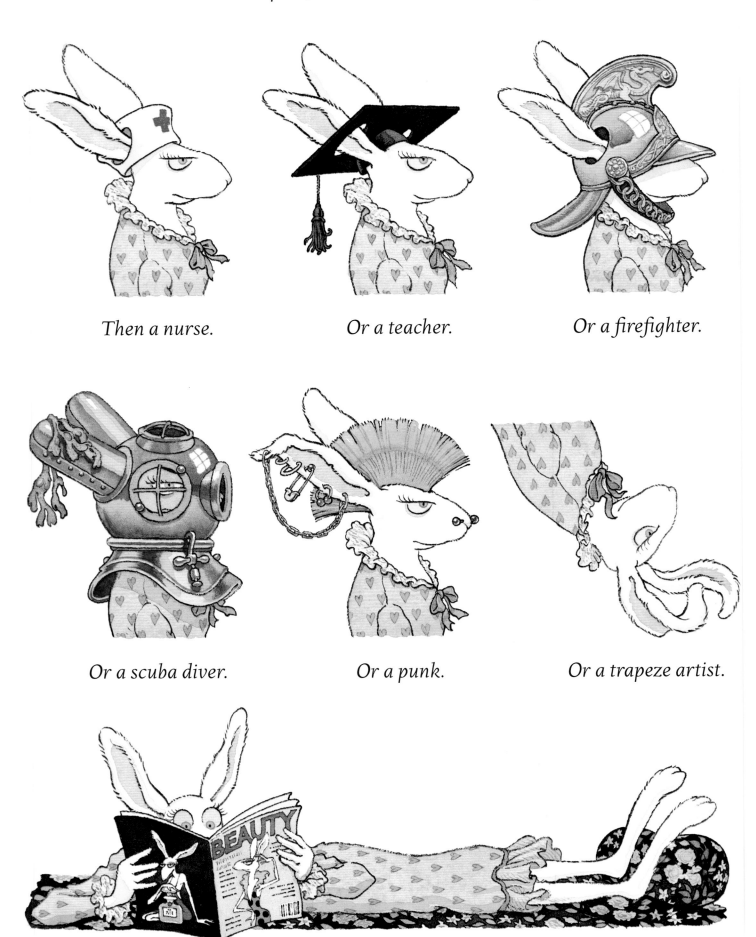

Then a nurse.

Or a teacher.

Or a firefighter.

Or a scuba diver.

Or a punk.

Or a trapeze artist.

Now she has decided to become a supermodel.

She spends all her time on the scale and refuses to swallow even a single bite.

1: Double carrot sandwich. 2: Carrot kebabs. 3: Carrot boats with carrot filling. 4: Carrots serpentine. 5: Chef's carrot. 6: Spicy carrot satay. 7: Purée of carrot greens with baby carrots. 8: Zigzag carrots. 9: "Grandmother's Hat" carrots. 10: "Battle of Trafalgar" carrots. 11: Carrot cocktail. 12: Carrot flan. 13: Log cabin carrots. 14: Carrot petit fours. 15: Carrot stew. 16: Carrot rum cake. 17: Eiffel Carrot. 18: Carrots stuffed with carrot greens. 19: Yin Yang carrots. 20: Race car carrots. 21: Carrots Apollo. 22: Carrot cookies. 23: Carrot surprise cake. 24: Carrot cupcakes. 25: Carrot saltimbocca. 26: Carrots en sarcophage. 27: Carrot fries. 28: Carrot bisque. 29: Carrot churros. 30: The Almighty Carrot Dragon. 31: "Jaws" carrots. 32: "Crazy bunny" carrots. 33: Carrots à la forestière. 34: Carrot cone. 35: Over-and-under carrots. 36: Carrot Charlotte with wild carrot purée. 37: Carrot rolls. 38: Carrot soufflé. 39: Carrot sashimi. 40: Carrot lasagna. 41: Carrots sans tops and tips. 42: Carrot chips. 43: Miniature carrot club sandwiches. 44: Sweet carrot macarons. 45: Carrot candy cane. 46: Carrots Robinson. 47: "Tea for Two" carrots. 48: Carrot-peas and carrots. 49: Steamed carrots. 50: Carrot toast.

Even though I've tried all the recipes from
100 Ways to Cook Carrots,

51: Carrot-top dumplings. 52: Valentine carrots. 53: Baby carrots. 54: Carrot salami. 55: Carrot donuts. 56: Carrot Kangaroo. 57: Carrots en papillotes. 58: Pickled carrots. 59: Carrot popsicles. 60: Carrot Yule Log. 61: Carrot roast. 62: "When the cat's away" carrots. 63: Grand Carrot Jello Tower. 64: Carrot fondue. 65: Soft-boiled carrot. 66: Fisherman's carrots. 67: "Free Willy" carrots. 68: Carrot nougat. 69: Caramel carrots. 70: "Trade Winds" carrots. 71: Sautéed carrots. 72: Carrot tea. 73: Carrot sorbet. 74: Carrot marmalade. 75: Carrots flambées. 76: The carrot recipe to give you strength and hairy armpits. 77: Carrot split. 78: Carrot juice. 79: R2D2 Carrot. 80: Carrot cotton candy. 81: Carrot taffy. 82: Elixir of carrot. 83: Carrots Brancusi. 84: Thumb carrot. 85: Carrots Buren. 86: Carrots à la Venice. 87: Japanese-style carrot skewer. 88: Carrots Napoleon. 89: Carrot-dog. 90: Easter Island carrots. 91: Greek carrots. 92: Carrots Luxor. 93: Carrot wedding cake. 94: Carrot and stick. 95: Carrot checkmate. 96: Accordion carrot. 97: "The Magic Flute" carrot. 98: Iron carrot. 99: Carrots cannonball. 100: Last chance carrots.

nothing will do.

Gilbert and George, the twins, are less of a worry.

They are wise and thoughtful boys,

interested in everything . . .

. . . and they know how to have fun with almost anything.

Betty is a little bit concerned about starting school.

But Mrs. Hare, the teacher, has assured us

that the class is lively and diverse, with tremendous potential.

My little Eliot sometimes seems to be quite advanced for his age.

Though sometimes not so much.
For Halloween, he insisted on wearing a bunny costume.

*The adorable baby of the family, Emily, is the spitting image of her father:
she bawls the whole blessed day.*

For a while now, a cat has also taken up residence here.

It is sneaky,

thieving,

energetic,

cowardly,

greedy,

and . . . transparent.

This is normal, my husband claims, since the cat is from Cheshire.
I don't care if it's from Cheshire, Hampshire, Yorkshire, or Anyshire —
I still don't want its dirty paws hanging around here!

Unfortunately, Eliot has become so fond of it
that I don't have the heart to throw it out . . .

. . . and so we've ended up adopting it.

If only it was just the cat! A young girl, from who knows where, turned up the other day. She seemed quite well-mannered, except for her unpleasant tendency to change size at the drop of a hat.

"Maybe we could hire her as a babysitter?" my husband suggested. A babysitter! Another one of his brilliant ideas! Who wants their children looked after by someone who doesn't know how to stay a reasonable size?

Thank goodness, after making me dizzy with her constant transformations, she left. I suspect the twins had something to do with that . . .

Here, everyone knows everyone else — and gossip runs wild.

When I buy a new hat, the whole town knows.

Except, of course, my husband, who never notices anything.

I might as well walk around with a bucket on my head.

It would be nice if he paid just a little attention to me every once in a while.

Sometimes I dream about how sweet it would be
to share some simple, happy moments together.

Sometimes I even imagine — how silly I am! — a world
in which men might help out with the housework . . .

But my husband has a lot of work to do at the palace . . .

. . . and he has to stay late quite often.

So that's it. My dear diary, now you know everything.
My life is quite different from what I once dreamed about.
I would have loved to be a writer. To invent stories full of marvelous
places and extraordinary characters. But how could I find inspiration
in my dull everyday life?

Time goes by and nothing changes. Cooking, cleaning, and looking
after my children take up most of my time. Today I'm 30 years old.
Does my husband even remember that it's my birthday?

NOTE FROM THE AUTHOR:

ooooo

If you leave your diary lying around,
someone may read it . . .